A JEW MUST DIE

Jacques Chessex

Translated from the French
by W. Donald Wilson

BITTER LEMON PRESS
LONDON

BITTER LEMON PRESS

First published in the United Kingdom in 2010 by
Bitter Lemon Press, 37 Arundel Gardens, London W11 2LW

www.bitterlemonpress.com

First published in French as *Un Juif pour l'exemple* by
Bernard Grasset, Paris in 2009

Bitter Lemon Press gratefully acknowledges the financial assistance
of Pro Helvetia, the Arts Council of Switzerland

swiss arts council
prohelvetia

© Éditions Grasset & Fasquelle, 2009
English translation © W. Donald Wilson, 2010

A CIP record for this book is available from the British Library

ISBN 978–1–904738–51-0

Printed in the United Kingdom by
JF Print Ltd, Sparkford, Somerset

I am the man that hath seen affliction by the rod of his wrath. He hath led me, and brought me into darkness, but not into light. Surely against me is he turned; he turneth his hand against me all the day.

Lamentations 3:1–3

1

When this story begins, in April 1942, in a Europe cast into fire and bloodshed by Adolf Hitler's War, Payerne, a fair-sized market town on the edge of the La Broye plain, not far from the border with Fribourg, is beset by dark influences. It had once been the capital of Queen Berthe, widow of Rodolphe II, King of Burgundy, who in the tenth century endowed it with an abbey church. Rural, well-to-do, the bourgeois town prefers to turn a blind eye to the recent decline of its industries and the people thereby reduced to poverty: five hundred unemployed to haunt it out of five thousand inhabitants born and bred.

The cattle and tobacco trades are the source of the town's visible wealth. But pork-butchery most of all. The pig in every shape and form: bacon, ham, trotters, hocks, sausage, sausage with cabbage and liver, head cheese, smoked chops, pâtés, ears, minced liver. The emblem of the pig dominates the town, lending it an amiable, contented air. With rustic irony the inhabitants of Payerne are called "red pigs". But dark currents flow unseen beneath the assurance and business bustle. Complexions are rosy or ruddy, the soil is rich, but covert dangers lurk.

The War is far off: such is the general view in Payerne. It concerns others. And in any case the Swiss Army ensures our safety with its invincible battle plan. Our elite Swiss infantry, our mighty artillery, our air force as effective as the Luftwaffe, and above all our impressive anti-aircraft defence with its 20-mm Oerlikon and 7.5-cm flak guns. Fortifications all across the difficult terrain, heavily armed strongholds, toblerone anti-tank lines and, if things should go wrong, our impregnable "national redoubt" in the mountains of the Vieux-Pays. It would take some cunning to catch us out.

And then, when evening falls, the blackout. Drawn curtains, closed shutters, every source of light obscured. But what is obscured, and by whom? What is there to hide? Payerne breathes and sweats in its bacon fat, tobacco and milk, the meat of its herds, the money in the Cantonal Bank, and the town's wine that must be fetched from Lutry on the shores of distant Lake Geneva, just as in the days of the abbey monks – the same wine that for almost a thousand years has brought solar inebriation to a capital set in its vanity and its lard.

In spring, when this story begins, all around is lovely, with an almost supernatural intensity that contrasts with the heinous events in the town. Remote countrysides, misty forests at dawn, smelling of chill wild creatures, game-rich valleys already filled with fog, the strum of the warm breeze on great oak trees. To the east the hills close in around the outlying houses; the rolling landscape unfolds in the green light, while on plantations, stretching as far as the eye can see, tobacco is springing up in the wind from the plain. And the beech woods, open woodlands, pine groves, thick hedges and bright coppices that crown the Grandcour hills.

But evil is astir. A powerful poison is seeping in. O Germany, the abominable Hitler's Reich! O Nibelung-en, Wotan, Valkyries, brilliant, headstrong Siegfried; I wonder what fury can be instilling these vengeful spirits from the Black Forest into the gentle woodlands of Payerne: the aberrant dream of some absurd Teutonic knights assailing the air of La Broye one spring morning in 1942, as God and a gang of demented locals are taken in, once again, by a brown-shirted Satan.

2

In 1939, when war breaks out, some of Payerne's five hundred unemployed are called up to serve in the federal army. The two hundred "unfit to serve" hang around miserably in cafés, living off dodges and petty crime. The crisis of the Thirties is not yet over, and it is a killer. The local economy is in a bad way. The Bank of Payerne fails. Several factories and workshops disappear, then a large brickworks, several mills, the Agricultural Distillery and the condensed-milk plant, employing over a hundred and fifty workers, male and female. Sinister-looking characters are seen roaming the roads and streets, wearing copper earrings and black kerchiefs knotted around scrawny necks. Beggars ring on doorbells. The cafés are filled with malcontents.

Dissatisfaction, poverty, rape, drunkenness and endless accusations are rife.

Who is to blame? The filthy rich. The well-to-do. The Jews and freemasons. They know how to line their pockets, especially the Jews, when factories are closing. Just look how prosperous they are, those Jews, with their cars, their furs and businesses with tentacles reaching everywhere, while we Swiss are dying of hunger. And to cap it all, this is *our* country. The Jews and the freemasons. Leeches, sucking our true blood.

There are several Jewish families in Payerne. One of them, the Bladts, originally from Alsace, owns the Galeries Vaudoises, a forerunner of the Monoprix department stores: goods from Paris, household articles, toys, good clothes and work clothes, on Main Street, in the centre of town, the only shop anywhere around that sells a range of merchandise. Several floors, twenty-odd employees. The Galeries' success and the business savvy of Jean Bladt, their owner and manager, spark the envy and then the ire of the town's small shopkeepers. Another Jew getting under our skin. Look what they've done in other places.

Other places. Other places means Germany; the persecution of the Jews there gives ideas to the big fat pork-eaters and Protestants – though no one will admit it, for here you live in the implicit, the sneer, the insinuation.

Jewish vermin. Cockroach Jews. Scheming Jews, a finger in every pie all over our economy, weaselling their way into politics, even into the law, the army. Just look at the cavalry, where Jews do so well.

Avenches, ten miles away in the direction of Berne, got a synagogue in the previous century. The community there is more active and more established than in Payerne. A stud farm and horse dealership. But the synagogue is to be closed, and nasty rumours are spreading through the ancient Roman countryside (the town was once a capital for Emperor Marcus Aurelius). *La Nation*, the organ of the Vaudois League, denounces the Jews of Avenches and Donatyre, a nearby village in which the presence of a Jewish family irks the editors of the extreme right-wing newspaper. Who should be entitled to breed and sell horses when our army needs them so badly in this time of war? Who should be profiting from it, instead of the Jewish scum sucking our local blood and marrow?

There is not much risk in pointing at the Jewish vampire. In Lausanne, as early as 1932, a group of lawyers, egged on by Marcel Regamey's Vaudois League, tried to have Jews excluded from the bar. Their demand was broadened to include all the liberal professions and the upper ranks of the army. Another schemer and agitator for the past several years has been Pastor Philippe Lugrin, until recently the incumbent of the parish of Combremont, a raving anti-Semite and member of the Vaudois League, then of the Front, and then of the National Union (which has chosen the district of La Broye to infiltrate the unemployed, the impoverished small farmers and workers in fear of losing their jobs). In the back rooms of cafés in Payerne and the surrounding countryside, this individual holds meetings violently inflamed by hatred of the Jew and the "Jewish International".

The Reverend Lugrin was recently relieved of his pastoral duties, less because of his ideas, which do not appear to bother the Church at all, than because he divorced the daughter of a powerful figure in Lausanne. However, the German Legation is looking on, and secretly puts him on its payroll. For Philippe Lugrin is able, ferociously cold-blooded and highly organized. Listing Vaudois and Swiss Jews, cataloguing their businesses and activities, enumerating their accomplices and backers, recording their addresses, phone numbers and car number plates, Lugrin agitates, denounces, caricatures and calls for a conspicuous example to be made. A familiar figure in the Nazi legation in Berne, and supported by it financially and logistically, this strange man of God interweaves in his diatribes enumerations of recent bankruptcies of honest, indigenous industries and the Torah, police reports and the business register, the *Protocols of the Elders of Zion*, the mythologies of ancient Europe and the theories of Alfred Rosenberg, the fascination of Dr Josef Goebbels and, above all, *Mein Kampf*. Again he calls for an example. Vengeance! Parasites! Kill the rats!

His public understands that a clean sweep is required to rid them without further delay of the breed responsible for their humiliation. Shouts and applause. *Deutschland über alles! Die Fahne hoch!* The recording of the Nazi anthem, which Lugrin has brought along in his little suitcase, crackles and booms from the bistro's gramophone. Tonight, behind closed frontiers, Europe lies in Hitler's grip. Stalingrad is still far off. Here, on the peaceful plain of La Broye, in the Café de la Croix Blanche, Le Cerf, or the Winkelried, every meeting held by Pastor Lugrin ends with a clicking of heels and the stiff-arm salute. Death to the Jews! *Heil Hitler!* O Führer, may you rule a thousand years over your resurgent Europe!

3

In Payerne the speeches of the Hitlerite pastor have fallen on fertile ground. Holding more and more meetings, stirring up the rancour and frustrations caused by the crisis, the efforts of the tempter Philippe Lugrin are crowned with success. In the back rooms where we have seen him at work, and often at night in disused sheds or abandoned brickworks, sometimes in a clearing in Invuardes forest lit by torches or adapted motorcycle headlamps, the cleric's lean frame, brusque gestures, head with slicked-down hair, little Goebbels-style spectacles, and then his words, coolly spoken but with a burning conviction you can sense beneath their icy surface, have galvanized his audience of the unemployed, embittered, disappointed peasants and impoverished, impotent, hot-headed swaggerers now keen to settle scores with the Jewish canker, the octopus, the tentacular monster, the international plot that is undermining our trade, taking over our banks, allied with Moscow, New York and London to erode our integrity, strangling us a day at a time.

In these remote countrysides the hatred of the Jew has a taste of soil mulled over in bitterness, turned over and ruminated, with the glister of pig's blood and the isolated cemeteries from where the bones of the dead still speak, of misappropriated inheritances, suicides, bankruptcies and embittered, frustrated bodies a hundred times humiliated. Hearts and groins have oozed a heavy broth into the black, age-old earth, mingling their thick humours in the opaque soil with the blood of herds of swine and horned cattle. The mind, or what remains of it, inflamed by murky family and political jealousies, is looking for a scapegoat to blame for all life's injustice and suffering, and finds it in the Jew, so different from us, with his prominent nose, olive complexion and crinkly hair on his broad skull. A Jew has a bank account and a big belly – nothing surprising in that. The Jew and his circumcision. The Jew that doesn't eat the way we do. The Jew grown fat from robbing us with his banks, pawnbroking and dealing in the cattle and horses he sells to our army. *Our* army!

A hereditary blending of the blood from animal and human carcasses bound to their rural destiny, dissolving in the earth of neglected graveyards. Lives brought to naught, dead folk who have never left this unbounded landscape, imprisoned, stupefied, ruminating: "I've been exploited. Robbed." Words full of hate.

How strange that these words should be heard again and again in the transparent light of these hills, in the idyllic radiance of early spring. At the base of the yellow limestone abbey church, the town goes on with life, as if the air and people's souls were not rent by any threat, by any danger. Each week at Payerne market, on the little square where the wind comes leaping from the plain, there are baskets of winter vegetables, rennet apples and little dried fruits; despite the "rationing", baskets of eggs, thick round cheeses, cream from the dairies, honey from woodland and meadow, fruit bottled in grape juice and walnut oil. The cutler's table, the abundance on the butchers' and delicatessen stalls, are shaded from the spring sun by orange canvas and tarpaulins, beneath which the filtered light casts a glow over the splendid meat. Always meat. From where would the warning come? As if the too rich soil of the surrounding countryside was fated to end in these bloody cuts of meat: sirloins, ribs, liver, dark red, with a glaze of purple ooze. While pig's heads, as if sculpted, grin from white dishes, one thinks of the capitals in the nearby church, wanted ten centuries before by a saintly queen for the serenity and constancy of her subjects.

4

In Payerne, in the Ischi brothers' garage opposite the Town Hall and the cool, mysterious deer park, the youngest of the brothers, Fernand Ischi, has been a member of the Swiss National Movement for the past several years. In Georges Oltramare of Geneva, this Fernand had found a thundering leader of the extreme right, a great beguiler, crafty tactician, unscrupulous orator, provocateur and troublemaker. Oltramare has one obsessive design: the victory of Nazi Germany, and then the extermination of the Swiss Jews. In Geneva, Fernand Ischi, an unskilled helper in the family garage and occasional repairer of bicycles and motorcycles, a ne'er-do-well exiled from the town of his birth, has followed this Nazi kingpin

Georges Oltramare from meeting to meeting and has fallen under his spell.*

Oltramare singles him out, flatters him and puts him in touch with Pastor Philippe Lugrin. There follow numerous enthusiastic meetings between the perverted theologian and the apprentice Nazi Gauleiter.

"Gauleiter?" you say. "Isn't that going a bit fast?"

From the age of sixteen, after leaving school, where he was an average student, inspired only by gym class, Fernand Ischi has been entranced by Germany, Hitler's seizure of power, the rise of Nazism and its violence. In 1936, during the Berlin Olympics, he saw Leni Riefenstahl's films in Geneva cinemas and developed a passion for the hard, clear propaganda ideal: the beauty of Aryan physiques, the banners, the nudity, the blond hair, the fanfares of Gothic trumpets, the blue eyes gazing up into the Führer's ecstatic gaze... Fernand Ischi is a mass of yearning and solitude. The blinkered mentality of his native town. The rarity of his prey. A strong gymnast and enthusiastic bodybuilder, Ischi overtrains his muscles and tests his strength in increasingly demanding exercises. Of medium height – "but Adolf Hitler's exactly", as he reminds anyone willing to listen – and already balding at the temples at thirty, but with a barrel-like chest, broad shoulders and biceps that bulge beneath his brown shirt, he makes quite an impression and, although married and the father of a boy and two girls, has developed a reputation as a Don Juan that makes up for his social failure. Involved for the time being in a close relationship with the female spy Catherine Joye, a member of the National Movement and an agitator, for whose activities and enthusiastic debauchery her husband Marcel Joye provides a cover, Fernand Ischi is the lover of a siren, the well-informed, efficient liaison operative from the Café Winkelried in Payerne, and certainly also of her young friend Annah, aged seventeen, whom he will soon bend abjectly to his fantasies. To the members of his party who are uneasy, and perhaps envious of these excesses, Fernand Ischi repeats with a superior smile Adolf Hitler's saying: "There's nothing finer than training up a young girl."

Fernand Ischi, along with twenty or so inhabitants of Payerne, has sworn fealty to the Nazi Party. He is a braggart, full of himself, but sly, practical, well-informed, consumed by hatred, by a desire for revenge and for power. He detests

Jews, but also hates and despises the burghers of Payerne who have witnessed his poor performance in school and his subjection, in the garage, to his brothers' authority. Since leaving school, while still very young, he has always carried a weapon, a Walther 7.65 that he flaunts to impress. To intimidate. To threaten. Once, in a club in the town where he goes drinking, Ischi shot at the bathing beauty on an advertisement for vermouth. He aimed at her breasts and vagina. Another evening, after one of Pastor Lugrin's meetings, he gives a ride on the pillion of his motorcycle to Georges Ballotte, aged nineteen, the apprentice mechanic from the garage. The two accomplices, both armed, speed off towards La Provençale, the Bladt family's house on the Corcelles road, where Fernand Ischi fires several shots at the windows and walls of the all too handsome residence. Getting up in haste, Jean Bladt tries to call the police: no answer; the station is empty. And the next morning, at daybreak: "It must have been the wind," says the duty policeman. "Or a cat. An owl. Or a hallucination. That's it. You must have been dreaming. It's hard to see who could get any fun out of firing a pistol at your house at past two in the morning."

With his frequent mistresses, Ischi does not disdain ritual games of domination. One relates that he whipped her, legs parted, with a Waffen SS belt. He poses, clicks his heels and makes the raised-arm salute over and over before the mirror. And he has his picture taken in Nazi uniform by Juriens the photographer.

"It's hard to see…" said the policeman in charge of the station at daybreak. But yes, they see. They'd rather cut out their tongues, rupture eyes and ears, than admit they know what is being plotted in the garage. In the back rooms of certain cafés. In the woods. At Pastor Lugrin's. The scheming, intriguing and networking by the German Legation in Berne providing inspiration and support for the Swiss Nazis, above all Oltramare in Geneva and Lugrin in the Vaud. And the activities of the SNM, the powerful, vindictive Swiss National Movement, the Payerne cell of which has been revived by Ischi, who rules it with the iron fist of a Gauleiter soon destined for power.

Following these exploits with the poster and the Bladt house, Fernand Ischi and Georges Ballotte, his apprentice, write anonymous threats and send them to Jewish families around Lausanne and La Broye. Then, on Lugrin's orders, they plan two attacks on the synagogues in Lausanne and Vevey. "We'll send it sky-high, their tabernacle!" sneers the sinister pastor, smoothing his brow with both hands, his gesture of serene satisfaction. These attacks will never be carried out for lack of time and local accomplices. In Vevey, and Lausanne especially, the Jewish community is more substantial and better organized than in Payerne. Anyway, the anonymous letters, intimidations, telephone threats, plans to dynamite or set on fire, all these activities will be ordered and overseen by Pastor Lugrin, who will continue to provide the conspirators in Payerne with lists and maps.

To relax properly in peace from his responsibilities, Fernand Ischi very often awakens the young Annah in the middle of the night and terrorizes her, forcing her to act out sadistic scenarios.

"On your knees, Annah. Let's pretend you're a Jewess. On your knees, Annah. You're a Jewess, Annah."

"You're completely crazy," says Annah.

She is naked. Trembling, she obeys.

The belt whistles, biting into the girl's back and thighs. Blood spurts. Kneeling by her, Ischi licks the blood that has flowed: "Your Jewess's blood, Annah, a sow's blood."

Beyond closed frontiers, very far and very near, the *Panzerdivisionen* and Luftwaffe have obliterated every defence. Poland has fallen, as have Czechoslovakia, Hungary, Romania, Belgium; France is occupied; Italy is an ally; Japan has joined in the dance; now the Panzers, the black, indestructible Panzers, have been thrown against Stalin. Death to Judeo-Bolshevism! Total victory is only weeks away. A few months at most. By the end of this year, 1942, all Europe, and Russia, will be in Hitler's grasp. Let his dominion begin. And let it be right here in Payerne that the first steps are taken towards Nazi rule in Switzerland, a dominion within his dominion, of which Gauleiter Ischi, with his party of brave men, will be the cleansing chief.

7 p.m., Monday 6 April 1942. The sun is setting in the sharp, buoyant, spring air. Ischi has taken his motorcycle and set out for the hills that dominate Payerne to the east. He stops in the hamlet of Trey. Now he is gazing

at the vast plain lit by scattered sunlight. What can he be thinking, Fernand Ischi, at this melancholy moment of spring, facing this expanse bathed in mist and the hills that rise and fall to the horizon at Surpierre, to the crests of the forests by Lucens? Is he moved to the depths of his spirit by the memory of his family, good people, loving people, on whom, by committing his hideous crime, he is about to inflict the greatest sorrow of their lives? So many friends have already turned their backs on him. His anguished wife has so often begged him to abandon his plan. And his children… their entire future. But at this word "future" Ischi feels a surge of energy; he baulks, gets a grip on himself and immediately reproaches himself with his moment of weakness. The future is the German victory. The future is the Northern Province with him as its Prefect, its unchallenged, efficient Gauleiter. The future is Adolf Hitler and the triumph of the New Order over a Europe rid of its vermin and united into a Great Reich. So what of these small hills, with these little evening vapours that soon dissolve from their outer edges? With a wave of his hand he dispels these old daydreams like the mists, gets back on his motorcycle, a rugged hero, and pays a visit to young Annah, her buttocks striped by the lashes from a belt, in the one-room apartment on Rue des Granges lent him by the waitress in the Winkelried.

Note:

Subsequently, living abroad in occupied France from 1941 to 1944, Georges Oltramare became a newsreader and presenter on the Nazi-controlled Radio-Paris. He had a regular spot under the name Dieudonné.

5

In 1942 several Jewish families are living in Payerne, including the Bladts, the Gunzburgers, who sell cloth and work clothes, and the Fernand Blochs, who have brought their parents from Alsace to live with them. Mme Bloch has to suffer the sarcastic, threatening remarks of the official in the municipal offices whenever their residence permit has to be renewed. Very often the Bloch's son is insulted and set upon on his way home from school. Stones are thrown at him; he is struck with tree branches. "Filthy Yid," shout the boys, whose efforts their parents continue with jeers and blows. Terrified, young Bloch goes to earth at home and refuses to return to school.

Meanwhile Pastor Lugrin will convince Ischi and his Nazis to act. The time is ripe for the band to set an example for Switzerland and for the Jewish parasites on its soil. So a really representative Jew must be chosen without delay, one highly guilty of filthy Jewishness, and disposed of in some spectacular manner. Threats and warnings. A good house-cleaning. Purification. A means to hasten the final solution. *Sieg heil!*

Only the victim is lacking. One of the Yids in Payenne? Jean Bladt tops the list. Anyway, like all these parasites, his turn will come. And the sooner the better. Avenches? That would create less of a sensation than Payenne, where they must strike hard, for it is to be the seat of the new government.

In the end the heinous choice falls on the devout, well-to-do Arthur Bloch, a Jewish cattle-dealer from Berne, well known to the farmers and butchers throughout the area, making him an obvious and exemplary victim. The next livestock fair will take place in Payenne on Thursday 16 April. Arthur Bloch will attend. That is where they must act. That will be the day to set a resounding example.

The idea comes from the Marmier brothers and their farmhand, Fritz Joss. But who are the Marmier brothers? In the garage, a disreputable group has quickly formed around Gauleiter Fernand, and among its members are two ruined small farmers, the brothers Max and Robert Marmier, and their burly farmhand Fritz Joss, a taciturn, strapping fellow from Berne, who blindly follows his masters. Fritz Joss is your perfect henchman, a hard, tireless worker. The Marmier brothers managed their farm poorly. A ferment of vengeance. They turned to carting, offering to convey provisions between farms, markets and the recently constructed barracks at the military airport, three miles outside town towards Grandcour. Business has improved somewhat over the past two or three years, but the Marmiers cannot get over the loss of their farms and fields. Still, they have bought a *rural*, a small farm building, in Payerne itself, on the old Rue-à-Thomas. As we shall see, these very modest premises will very soon take on a sordid significance in this story – a story infused with the poisonous breath of Pastor Philippe Lugrin, the evil genius of the Movement, who perpetually adds new names to the list of Jews to be terrorized, who regularly summons Fernand Ischi to his office in Prilly to dictate to him orders from the SNM, who, on three long evenings each week, harangues and indoctrinates the Movement's members and sympathizers in Payerne and around, and who acts as liaison with the German Legation.

On Saturday 4 April, he summons Fernand Ischi to Prilly. "The time has come," Lugrin tells him. "We can't wait any longer. *Heil Hitler!*"

Elated, as he is on each of his visits to Prilly, Fernand Ischi looks at the wall with its Nazi trophies, decorations and large portrait of Hitler in his brown uniform, Iron Cross on his chest, wearing the Nazi armband. On the wall and on the bookshelves he can see the photos of Rosenberg, the theoretician of Nazism, Himmler, Albert Speer, Dr Josef Goebbels and the indomitable Riefenstahl. To beguile him, the pastor invites him to sit opposite him in his study shaded by a lime tree with fresh green leaves, offers him a packet of Laurens Reds, Ischi's favourite cigarettes, and opens a bottle of Rhine wine, a gift from the German Legation. Lugrin approves the choice of Arthur Bloch. He smooths his forehead with the long, slim fingers of both hands, and smiles at Ischi, who is on edge. "Good plan," he says flatteringly. "Clever strategy. In Payerne everyone knows Arthur Bloch. A household name! And before long the town's precious sacrificial victim!"

Fernand Ischi returns home from Prilly highly elated and brimming with pride. At last, the proof expected of him. A Jew, as an example. Recognition. Now there will be no mistake. Time for the Jewish community in Switzerland to realize what awaits it. And just at the right moment, you might say. On 16 April Arthur Bloch is disposed of. Adolf Hitler's birthday falls on 20 April. They can be sure the German Legation will announce the glad news to the Führer that very day; he'll remember the gift when the New Order, now so close at hand, arrives.

6

Arthur Bloch is sixty. Wide mouth, thick lips, round cheeks and a high forehead surmounted by a head of smooth hair, still black and shining, neatly parted on the left. Medium height, stoutish, always soberly dressed with a waistcoat and black tie, his suit jacket buttoned all the way. He has his clothes made by M. Isaac Bronstein, a tailor in the capital, so that he can have many inside pockets in his jackets and overcoats. Not liking to be burdened with an attaché case or briefcase, he always carries the large banknotes needed for his purchases tucked in his wallet. A watch chain bare of trinkets lies across his stomach.

Deaf in his left ear, Arthur Bloch bends his head when in company to catch the conversation. Often has a Sonotone hearing aid in his left ear. Invariably wears a black or very dark grey felt hat, round in shape, and rarely ventures out without his willow walking stick gripped in a fist that gleams with sweat, for when he is buying he has the habit of prodding and poking the animals in the ribs and hindquarters with his stick in order to judge them better.

Arthur Bloch was born in 1882 in Aarberg, Canton of Berne, the only boy in the family and elder brother to four girls. Arthur Bloch was nine when his father died in 1891. His mother sent him to learn the language at the French Institute; after that he did his military service in Lucerne and Thun, in the cavalry – horses already. In 1914, when war broke out, he served in the federal army, in the dragoons. It was then he lost the hearing in one ear.

In 1916, aged thirty-four, he took over the cattle dealership belonging to his uncle, Jakob Weil. The business prospered. In 1917 he married Myria Dreyfus, a girl from Zurich, and the couple set up house in Berne, at 51 Monbijoustrasse, an elegant street not far from the railway station. The Blochs were still living there in 1942.

Their first child died in infancy. Then, in December 1921, Liliane Désirée came into the world, and in March 1925, her younger sister, Éveline Marlise.

Arthur Bloch was a kind, generous, even-tempered man. Rabbi Messinger would speak of his calm manner. And Georges Brunschwig, president of the Jewish community in Berne, would recall Arthur Bloch's attachment to Switzerland, his father having become a citizen of the country and of the Canton of Berne at Radelfingen, near Aarberg, in 1872.

A cattle-dealer for more than twenty-five years, Arthur Bloch is a familiar figure at livestock markets in La Broye and makes regular business trips to Oron and Payerne – but it is Payerne he prefers, for he is personally acquainted there with all the farmers and butchers who attend on such occasions.

Arthur Bloch usually covers the short distance between Monbijoustrasse and the railway station on foot, stepping out to the rhythmic tap of his stick. He gets into the first train to La Broye, which reaches Payerne via Avenches. He likes this ninety-minute trip through the stretches of meadows and valleys still filled with mist in the early-morning light.

Arrival in Payerne at 6:18. Chestnuts in bloom, silken hills, bright weather, all the more beautiful since threatened from within and without. But Arthur Bloch is unaware of the danger. Arthur Bloch does not sense it.

At the fair, purchases are settled in cash, in full. No complications, nothing on paper. Merely a handshake. Arthur Bloch's wallet is heavy with the large notes with which he is going to pay for the red cows and bullocks he will pick out on the square. He is respected, he pays well; he willingly downs the glass of white wine poured for him at the fair itself or in the cowshed, sealing the deal and showing that the door is open to future transactions. He will also sit at a table in the cafés where his customers are drinking: the Vente, the Croix-Blanche, the Cerf, the Lion d'Or. He knows a lot of folk, buys his round and jots down new appointments. Flushed faces, sweaty brows, big hands, the smoke of Fivaz cigars and Fribourg pipes, waistcoats buttoned over wallets swollen by excellent deals. And all these voices with their heavy accent, exclamations and cries, excited and heated after several hours spent drinking Belletaz wine.

Afterwards Arthur Bloch takes the train back to Berne, and returns home, at peace with himself, to the house on Monbijoustrasse, where Myria has prepared an evening meal that the couple consumes in tranquillity, obedient to a law that Arthur never breaks.

7

At dawn on Thursday 16 April it is chilly; a light breeze is blowing on Payerne. By seven o'clock the farmers have tethered their beasts on Market Square to the wide metal railings that clank whenever the cows, bullocks and bulls pull on their halters and chains. Armed with metal shovels and large willow brooms, the stable lads collect the dung and throw it into the cart parked for the purpose at the railway-station end of the square, beside the train track, beneath the chestnut trees already in full leaf.

The animals' coats, hindquarters and nostrils steam in the cold air. The cattle low and bellow. A small herd is unloaded from a red-painted wagon, swelling the already considerable number of animals tied up there

– almost 160 head in all, for this is the first market of the year and no one wants to miss it.

On this Thursday 16 April 1942, Arthur Bloch arrives on Market Square at 8 a.m. He greets his acquaintances cheerily and chats with Thévoz from Missy, Avit Godel from Domdidier, Bruder the butcher and Bosset, Jules Brasey and, of course, Losey, from Sévaz. He spends some time looking at the animals brought by Émile Chassot from Villaz-Saint-Pierre, a splendid pair of red bullocks with white horns and glossy coats; their bluish nostrils are moist; they are well shaped in the neck, broad in the belly, with full haunches, promising meat of high quality. Twenty-five years as a cattle-dealer have not exhausted Arthur Bloch's curiosity. He likes to see, feel, smell and prod the animals he is buying in order to resell, sometimes coming across them at other fairs. With the point of his stick he presses on the flank of one of the animals from Villaz-Saint-Pierre, reaches out a hand, moves back to feel its haunch and gently strokes its neck… Arthur Bloch is deliberate, never peremptory or imperious. Unruffled and perspicacious, he displays the same wise caution as the local farmers. Rubbing shoulders with them, despite his difference he has long felt at one with them, that they esteem and respect him.

Something Arthur Bloch has failed to notice, too busy examining and buying bullocks from Godel, Chassot, Jules Brasey and Losey from Sévaz, is that for the past half-hour a silent little group of men in leather jackets, with blank expressions, are furtively moving around the fair without ever losing him from view. At first they kept their distance, but now they have come closer and are watching him.

They are the band from the garage. The Nazis of Ischi's Party: Ischi himself, the ringleader, the apprentice Georges Ballotte, the two Marmiers, Max and Robert, and the brawny farmhand, Fritz Joss.

But the conspirators know they have been noticed, and become uneasy.

"We're too obvious," says Ischi. "We stand out too much. I'm going back to the garage. Diversion. Max, you go and have a drink to see what they're saying in the cafés. Robert, with Ballotte and Fritz, you bring the Yid to Rue-à-Thomas, and dispatch him there. I'll join you with the orders."

This leaves Robert Marmier, the apprentice, and Fritz Joss, the farmhand. Suddenly Robert makes up his mind and speaks to Arthur Bloch just as he is putting his hand in his wallet to pay for the heifer he has just bought from Cherbuin of Avenches.

"Monsieur Bloch, if you don't mind…"

But Arthur Bloch chats with Cherbuin, then Brasey and then Losey. He goes off with them to look at some other animals, haggles, prods with his stick. Time is passing. It is a quarter to ten. It is beginning to grow hot on Market Square; the three plotters are sweating.

"This time, here goes," says Robert.

Again they approach Arthur Bloch.

"Good day, Monsieur Bloch," says Robert in a loud voice, for he has noticed the Sonotone, and the way Arthur Bloch strains to catch what he is saying.

Then he continues at the top of his lungs: "M. Bloch, my brother has a cow to sell. It's on Rue-à-Thomas, in the cowshed just round the corner."

"Rue-à-Thomas," repeats Arthur Bloch, suspecting nothing.

He is merely surprised that the animal is not on the square with the others.

"My brother didn't have time to bring her. He was sick this morning. But the animal's in good health! She's a grand beast, Monsieur Bloch. Healthy. A good milker. And my brother wants to sell her."

Arthur Bloch is tempted. He agrees. The two men set off under the now very warm sun; Ballotte joins them, and the farmhand completes the group.

8

They reach Rue-à-Thomas. On the way, no one has spoken. Arthur Bloch still suspects nothing. Is he tired? Jaded after the morning's good business? It seems surprising that such a level-headed man should be so lacking in discernment towards Robert Marmier, a failed, degenerate farmer, or the farmhand with his uncouth features, and especially young Ballotte, whose loutish exterior should have made him uneasy. But there is no logic in death. When he enters the cowshed on Rue-à-Thomas, Arthur Bloch is unaware, fails to *sense*, that the most horrible butchery awaits him.

There are only two cows to be seen, something unusual for a working farm. Yet Arthur Bloch still feels no disquiet.

As the four men enter the dark cowshed, one of the cows turns her head towards them, pawing the ground, rattling her chain. Obviously taken aback, Arthur Bloch hasn't expected to find such a fine animal.

"This is the one," says Robert Marmier, pointing his flashlight at her.

A fawn, almost reddish beast, long in the back, with full flanks above a distended udder with its coat of downy hair. The air is heavy with smells of moist belches, saliva and tenderly sexual milk. The female's eye gleams in the sunlight from the window and the flashlight beam turned on her.

Remaining silent for a long moment, Arthur Bloch probes her flanks and white underbelly with his hand and stick.

"And how much are you asking for this marvel?" he says at last, as if in a dream.

"Two thousand four hundred," says Robert.

"Two thousand," counters Arthur Bloch, suddenly waking up.

"Two thousand, two thousand, I couldn't…"

"And I can't offer a franc more."

The haggling has begun. Robert Marmier gets carried away. Ballotte and Fritz are furious at so much zeal. "We'd decided we'd bash him right away!" Robert is going too far. Arthur Bloch, tempted by the animal for sale, and wily as he is, pretends to pull out.

"Too bad. She's not for me." Then he adds, disappointed, "That's what I said, that's the way it is. I can't offer a franc more."

He shakes Robert's hand, turns away, reaches the door.

Georges Ballotte and Fritz Joss are torn between anger and the relief felt by those who are not as tough as they think. Robert, very pale, leans against the wall.

But Arthur Bloch is tempted. The cow's a good one, it's a reasonable deal. He walks a few yards down the street, allows five minutes to go by, then retraces his steps and re-enters the cowshed. It is 10:35. The three accomplices are taken by surprise.

"So, this cow," says Arthur Bloch. "I'll do my best for you. Fifty francs more, and I'll take her."

"Two hundred," says Robert Marmier, panicking, as if to postpone the inevitable. Arthur Bloch laughs.

"Are you trying to ruin me! No, that's too much. Too bad. She's not for me."

For the second time he takes his leave, pulls down his hat, slowly goes outside.

The three accomplices are aghast. Ballotte swears at Marmier: "Are you out of your mind, or what?"

"He'll be back," says Robert. "And this time we'll do for him."

Robert is right. The cowshed door has been left open. It is now almost eleven o'clock, and the light from outside is blinding as Arthur Bloch's heavy tread is heard on Rue-à-Thomas. For the third time, to the stupefaction of the three men, Arthur Bloch enters the cowshed, where he is sealing his death warrant.

Hardly has Arthur Bloch approached when Ballotte gives a push in the back of the terrified farm labourer Fritz, who is holding a heavy iron bar in his right fist.

"Hit him," spits Ballotte.

Deaf in one ear, Arthur Bloch has heard nothing.

Fritz Joss hesitates, standing looking at the nape of the Jew's neck and his large frame, as he again feels out the cow for sale, probing, muttering, up against the animal.

How should he strike, under the hat, or at the fat nape of his neck? Suddenly Fritz Joss feels the muzzle of the apprentice's revolver against his ribs. Ballotte prods him with the weapon:

"Party's orders. Kill him. Get on with it! Kill the swine!"

Joss the colossus raises the iron bar and brings it down with all his strength on the Jew's head; Bloch crumples to the ground, jerking convulsively, eyes rolling upwards, foaming at the lips, while a broken cry issues with the remaining breath of his large, prostrate, shuddering frame. His hat has rolled into the sawdust. Arthur Bloch is still moaning.

"He's not dead yet, the bastard," hisses Ballotte, bringing the muzzle of his revolver to his smooth pate.

The forehead is pale, shining with sweat. A moan, accompanied by rattles in his throat. Ballotte fires. Bloch's body collapses to the ground. A trickle of blood comes from his mouth.

"He's dead," says Marmier.

"Good riddance," sneers Ballotte. They await their leader's orders.

9

It is 11:15. In the sweltering cowshed the three men are covered in sweat. Bloch's body fills the short walkway between the stalls; his face has set stiff in the sawdust and straw, a translucent white like candle wax, as one of the killers would say during the investigation. Ballotte leans over the corpse.

"A dead man stinks," he mumbles.

"A Jew most of all," says Marmier.

"That's not the end of it," says Ballotte. "They told us to get rid of a Yid. So what about this big carcass? What are we going to do with this hunk of lard?"

"We could dissolve it in hydrochloric acid," says Marmier. "I buy it by the pint from the hardware shop to use in my septic tanks; they won't suspect anything."

"It'd take too long," decides Ballotte. "With the size of fatty here, it'd take at least three days. We can't afford to let him dissolve. The filthy swine."

It is then that Ischi comes in, followed by Max. Now the whole gang is there. It is 11:20. The five men are sweating in their leather jackets.

"Great work," says Ischi. He goes across to the dead man, bends over the body, laughs and launches a kick at the corpse. "*Heil Hitler!*"

"*Heil Hitler!*" echo the four others, their spirits lifting.

"What now?" asks Ballotte.

"Now we get rid of him."

"Hydrochloric acid?" Robert Marmier ventures again.

"Idiot!" exclaims Ischi. "You know very well it's too slow. Is there an axe anywhere around?"

Robert and the others have turned pale.

"Or a saw?" Ischi goes on. "Butcher's knives?"

"I've got the necessary," mutters Robert.

"Get to work then!" orders Ischi. "Fritz, you're the strongest. You cut up the body. The head, arms and legs, and remember to cut the legs in two! Then deal with the trunk. It won't be easy, with his size. Look at that paunch. The bastard! Getting fat like that at our expense."

The four men listen approvingly. Robert produces the tools. The axe, a solid saw, a long butcher's knife.

"We'll have to undress him first," says Ischi. "And divide up his cash. I'll work it out. The biggest share to the Party. I'll look after everything. His clothes, no problem, we'll burn them in the forest. We've found a place, Max and me."

"And the body?" asks Ballotte. "What are we going to do with the bits?"

"I'll look after everything," repeats Ischi. "We'll put all the bastard's bits in milk cans and sink them in the lake off Chevroux. I know a fisherman in the harbour there. I've already arranged to borrow his biggest boat. That's for this evening. After dark. Three hundred yards offshore, no one'll bother us. Heh! Heh! The fish'll do the rest."

10

On Rue-à-Thomas, in the Marmier brothers' cowshed, the killers have set about their gruesome task. After undressing the dead man, they hold the corpse by the four limbs and carve, saw and slice into it: first the hands, then the arms, the thick legs and the head, which gives them some trouble because the ligaments in the neck refuse to part and two of them are needed to tear it from the massive trunk.

Fritz Joss takes charge, thankful for the dreadful work, as if it afforded a kind of respite. The saw scrapes as it cuts into the Jew's bone. Fritz doesn't flinch, for he is used to this, having worked in a butcher's shop as an apprentice cutter and sliced up several animals, a trusted worker for other bosses. The teeth of the saw bite, the butcher's knife slices, separating the groin, armpits and arms.

Blood flows abundantly; splinters of bone fly, and shreds of flesh. To cover the sounds of butchering, Max chops some wood in front of the door, whistling and bawling one of Fernandel's songs:

Ignace, Ignace,
It's a little name I love,
Ignace, Ignace.
It's nice; it fits me like a glove.

It is 12:30. Max goes to fetch the three milk cans and sets them down in the cowshed, trying not to vomit. The stench of blood, lymph and fat is unbearable in the heat of the shed.

"You can't breathe in here," exclaims Ballotte. "Hurry up and finish, Fritz. We're beginning to have enough of dealing with this Yid."

Fritz Joss staggers in his effort. But the trunk resists. They have to turn it round and round to see where best to attack it. Finally they decide to chop it lengthwise with the axe. The breastbone divides and the spine and ribs are split. The job is done. One Jew less on Swiss soil.

Hastily they cram the stumps, head and half the trunk into the first container; the other half goes into the second can, along with the arms and hands, and, lastly, the legs into the third. But it is difficult to stuff them in completely, and the feet stick out, pathetic signals of distress; even in the deep waters of Lake Neuchâtel, they will rise to the surface at night, surrounded by squalling coots and seagulls. But what do a Jew's two feet matter? The order to kill has been carried out. Dominion is nigh. *Heil Hitler!*

11

In the meantime four animals have remained tethered to the railing in the market square with no one to take them away. They are the Godel, Brasey and Losey bullocks, and Cherbuin of Avenches's heifer, all bought by Arthur Bloch earlier this morning and now bellowing in the oppressive heat.

At 12:30 Charly Bruder the butcher takes a first look at the situation; he recognizes the animals and remembers who bought them. Where can Arthur Bloch have gone? But Bruder the butcher is not too worried: Bloch must have gone for a drink with one of his clients; he'll be back any time soon.

At one o'clock the animals are still bellowing, crazed by the sun. Charly Bruder decides to move them into the shade.

But there is still no sign of Arthur Bloch. At 3:00, Bruder the butcher and a few farmers emerging from the cafés decide to alert the police. "Arthur Bloch? He'll have taken the opportunity to get up to some mischief. In some hotel. Or in the forest. He'll turn up, don't you worry."

That evening, in Berne, Myria Bloch is worried, for her husband has not come home. Sensitive and highly strung, she has felt uneasy all day, and now she is panicking. She phones one of her daughters in Zurich, then calls a lawyer in Berne – a family friend, a member of the community. He will act first thing in the morning. First, call the police. Get things moving. Then hire Auguste-Christian Wagnière, the private detective from Lausanne, known for his doggedness and sound instincts. What is more, Wagnière enjoys the confidence of the local police and sometimes works with them; he knows the countryside inside out, is aware of Pastor Lugrin's comings and goings and of the Nazi agitation in Payerne. He suggests to Myria Bloch and her daughters that they place an announcement in the two local newspapers, *Le Démocrate* and *Le Journal de Payerne*, accompanied by photographs of Arthur Bloch and offering a reward for useful information.

Meanwhile Ischi, the gang's leader, has no time to waste. By the evening of the 16th, the dismembered body of the Jew Bloch is submerged in the lake off Chevroux. No worries there, he won't come up again. Next, dispose of his clothing. And share things out. His wallet? It contains five thousand Swiss francs, a lot of money for the time. Ischi divides them up: four thousand francs for the Party, just over four hundred for himself, and the rest divided between Ballotte and the Marmiers. Fritz Joss, the farm labourer who wielded the iron bar and butcher's knives, gets only twenty francs.

Then they will burn the suit, waistcoat and underwear at Neyrvaux, in a cave in the woods. *La grotte aux chauves-souris* – Bat Cave. It is not far from Vers-chez-Savary, a remote hamlet. Fernand Ischi and his gang have often used it as a hide-out. Max Marmier gets on the motorcycle pillion, holding the clothes and a few objects. Lights out, they speed towards the woods. There, the clothes, hat and stick, even the Sonotone, are thrown in a heap on the black earth and lit with a cigarette lighter. But the cave is damp, the fire fails to catch properly, and the clothes will not burn. Never mind. We mustn't get caught. Just the other evening, when we were scouting the place out, those two boys that saw us. We'll deal with them if we have to. Meanwhile let's not hang around. A little earth to cover things, a few pebbles, a pile of dead leaves – no one's going to come poking around here.

Ischi the ringleader and Max Marmier get back on the motorcycle and ride back to Payerne in the darkening inky night.

12

Late that night Fernand Ischi visits young Annah in the little room she rents on Rue des Granges, fondles her, takes his whip to her and makes her cry out until dawn.

Friday 17 April, Saturday 18 and Sunday 19: still no news of Arthur Bloch. But the most diverse rumours, lewd jokes, insinuations and gossip are rife in the cafés of Payerne. Arthur Bloch's elder daughter comes to Berne to give her mother support. The younger says she is on her way. Myria has eaten nothing since Thursday, and is surviving thanks to her doctor's injections.

On Monday 20 April, in Berlin, Wilhelm Furtwängler conducts Beethoven's Ninth Symphony to celebrate Adolf Hitler's birthday. In the presence of the leaders of the

Nazi regime, dignitaries' families and representatives of industry and the diplomatic corps, the Führer celebrates reaching the age of fifty-three. Josef Goebbels, Propaganda Minister of the Reich, marks the glorious occasion.

On Tuesday 21 April and Wednesday 22 April, the Bloch family's announcement appears, first in the *Journal de Payerne*, and the following day in *Le Démocrate*:

MISSING PERSON

The public is advised of the disappearance of M. Arthur BLOCH, cattle-dealer, b. 1882, resident in Berne, last seen on Market Square in Payerne on Thursday 16 April 1942.

Description: height approx. 5′7″, rather stout, clean-shaven, wearing a small Sonotone hearing aid; grey-beige coat, grey hat, probably carrying a walking stick.

Anyone able to provide information of any kind is asked to convey it immediately to the investigating judge, District of Payerne-Avenches. The family is offering a reward of 1,000 francs to anyone providing information leading to the discovery of this person or helping to establish the circumstances of his disappearance.

The announcement is accompanied by two quite clear photographs of Arthur Bloch – on the left, dressed in a suit and white shirt, with a white silk handkerchief in his breast pocket, taken against a strange black background that already consigns him to another world. In the one on the right, wearing his hat down over his eyebrows, he has the look of some heavy-featured aviator or an American banker in a 1920s silent movie.

Several people are heard from over the next few days. Arthur Bloch was spotted in the train to Berne: the same heavy build, the same clothes, but the missing man was fair-haired. Could Bloch have dyed his hair? Another confuses him with a certain Braun, a cattle-dealer from Basle who stayed at the Hôtel des Alpes in Payerne, but M. Braun isn't Jewish. Another confused him with a Monsieur Dreyfus, who also stayed at the Alpes. Others had come across him in Boulex woods, in the company of a woman. And others in the Hôtel de la Gare, with the same woman. The most useful evidence is provided by two young boys from the hamlet of Vers-chez-Savary, who had found some dark clothes, a hat, a stick and a Sonotone – a sad little list – in an isolated cave. These seem to have been the same youngsters who had spotted Fernand Ischi and Max Marmier reconnoitring the place a few days before.

At last a serious search begins. Wagnière gets his people moving. In Payerne, where the police have dispatched investigators, tongues have begun to wag, rumours and suspicions have acquired direction. The Nazis were the killers. The Fifth Column. The vice tightens. No doubt remains. It was the garage Gauleiter.

But curiously, instead of horror at the disappearance, or the uneasiness it spreads, inspiring compassion or sadness, in the cafés there is still sniggering, coarse jokes and loaded comments about "Jewry", "profiteering" and "parasitic" businesses. Copies of *Gringoire* and *Je suis partout* continued to circulate among prominent citizens. Never, since Hitler arrived on the scene and the Kristallnacht persecutions, has such a welling of hatred towards Jews been witnessed. And even those who would denounce Fernand Ischi and his gang at the trial still mock the Jews and their age-old terrors. A cattle-dealer has disappeared? An interesting turning of the tables: that's what people think in Payerne, awaiting further developments with a snigger.

13

Friday 24 April, 8 a.m. The weather is mild over Payerne: cool air, birdsong and bird calls from the lilacs and lime trees already in bloom. On the Corcelles road, a squad of Swiss national police and two constables from Payerne are waiting for Fernand Ischi at the Riollaz Bridge, which crosses the railway line among rusting warehouses, abandoned workshops and the premises of the Beauregard brewery. Further north, across the countryside, run rails nostalgic for trains whose locomotives belch black clouds of smoke. Further up the street, Ischi is about to leave home. Punctual, dapper, erect, he strides towards the policemen. And he is most likely armed. They caution him. Ischi does not resist. He is put in a holding cell in the town's jail.

He is searched. On him they find a firearm, the indispensable Walther 7.65, a few keys, several passports, an identity card, thirteen ration coupons, an open packet of Laurens Red cigarettes, five Disch caramels, a ticket for the Swiss Romande lottery, two letters postmarked Berne and two Nazi propaganda booklets.

Close-shaven, hair cut short, prominent ears facing forwards. Jacket and trousers of the latest fashion, of combed grey-green wool, very close-fitting, with a half-belt in the back to lend a military look. Laced shoes of a casual style, light-brown leather, with thick crêpe soles. Oddly, a green Tyrolean felt hat, tilted back on his head, gives him this morning the air of a guard or delivery man from the Berghof or Berchtesgaden. And a persistent scent of eau de Cologne.

Yes, he's an anti-Semite and has never concealed the fact. Yes, he thought that liquidating a Swiss Jew would provide a conspicuous example. And anyway, to hell with you, your police and your laws. In any case, Germany will have us out within the next few weeks. Do you think the Legation will allow us to be humiliated? He heard about Bloch's death from the newspapers. But yes, it was he, the leader, Fernand Ischi, Party chief and Gauleiter, who ordered the Marmier brothers to bring the Jew to Rue-à-Thomas and kill him there. He knows nothing about cutting up the carcass. But if they did it, they were right. The fat swine! No pity. He makes no mention of Georges Ballotte or Fritz Joss. The Jew's dismembered body has been sunk in Lake Neuchâtel.

Early that afternoon two senior police officers, Inspectors Jaques and Jaquillard, arrive in Chevroux by car, escorted by a squad of motorcycle police. The light is idyllic on the spring shoreline. Two of the sinister milk cans are resting on the bottom, four metres deep. From the third, floating half submerged, a man's feet protrude, surrounded by squalling gulls. Along with the legs, they find half of the trunk, split lengthwise, and the intestines, lungs and heart. The police inspectors give the order for the three containers to be conveyed to the hospital in Payerne.

14

The arrests of the other conspirators take place over the next thirty hours. The two youngsters from Vers-chez-Savary have recognized the motorcyclists from the *grotte aux chauves-souris*. Fritz Joss is arrested at Grosse Pierre Farm, near the military airfield, on the property of the Marmier parents. The Marmier brothers are found in their lairs at Grosse-Pierre and on Rue-à-Thomas. Ballotte is taken at his parents' house; his mother is a washerwoman, his father a warehouseman in the arsenal.

In front of the now closely guarded lock-up, the same crowd that had cast such a sarcastic eye on the search, accompanied by base suggestions and anecdotes, now hurls insults at the accused and calls for the maximum sentence. The dismembering of the body and dumping it in the waters off Chevroux have impressed peoples' imaginations and elicited stupefaction. An infectious mood of disapproval sweeps through this town of butchers and sausage-makers. Before the displays in butchers' windows, the fearful population suffers an onset of attraction and repulsion that intensifies the emotion, along with a kind of collective guilt that will long endure in the conscience of Payerne. The town's emblem – the cheerful, portly pig with broadly laughing snout, displaying its pink belly – the very trademark takes on an obscene, cynical, perverted look, for it recalls a different flesh, sacrificed and defiled for an odious cause. When the savage martyrdom of Arthur Bloch is mentioned, nearly everything, even the Jewish law, with its total prohibition of pork, is evoked by antithesis in a cruel symmetry of opposites: "They killed that Jew and cut him up like a pig in an abattoir." In its guilt, Payerne juxtaposes and merges the example of a Jew and pork meat, the Wailing Wall and the pig butcher's cleavers. O Jeremiah, melancholy prophet, you already spoke of the scandal: *The Eternal was unto me as a bear lying in wait, and as a lion in secret places. He hath turned aside my ways, and pulled me in pieces: he hath made me desolate.*

15

What is horror? When the philosopher Jankélévitch proclaims the entire crime of the Holocaust to be "imprescriptible", he forbids me to speak of it exempt from that edict. Imprescriptible. That can never be forgiven. That can never be paid for. Nor forgotten. Nor benefit from any statute of limitations. No possible redemption of any kind. Absolute evil, for which there can be no absolution ever.

I am telling a loathsome story, and feel ashamed to write a word of it. I feel ashamed to report what was said: words, a tone of voice, deeds that are not mine but that I make mine, like it or not, when I write. For Vladimir Jankélévitch also says that complicity is cunning and that repeating the slightest anti-Semitic sentiment or deriving some amusement or caricature from it, or putting it to some aesthetic purpose, is already, in itself, inadmissible. He is right. Yet it is not wrong of me, having been born in Payerne and spent my childhood there, to explore events that have never ceased to poison my memory and left me ever since with an irrational sense of sin.

I was eight years old when these events took place. In high school I sat next to Fernand Ischi's eldest daughter. The son of the officer commanding the police station who arrested Ischi was a pupil in that same class. So was the son of Judge Caprez, who would preside over the trial of Arthur Bloch's murderers. My father was principal of the high school and the Payerne elementary schools; since Ballotte had been a pupil of his, he was interviewed as a witness during the preparations for the trial. He was President of the *Cercle de la Reine Berthe*, a democratic, violently anti-Nazi club, and was himself on the list of future victims of the garage gang, after Jean Bladt and his children. At home, at school during breaks, in the shops, in the streets, loaded words fuelled the uneasiness. I remember the Nazi songs, Hitler's rants, the Wehrmacht brass bands broadcast over

Market Square at midday by loudspeakers and all the cars in the garage drowning the church bells, when school was out.

Saturday 25 April 1942. Since dawn the five accused have been under lock and key in the Bois-Mermet detention centre in Lausanne. The examination of the case can begin. The trial date has been set less than six months away; it is to open in the Payerne courthouse on 15 February 1943 and will last five days. Presiding judge: Marcel Caprez. The accused (whose lawyers – one of them, especially arrogant, from Geneva – are paid by the German Legation) go into sordid details. Confronted with the implements used in the butchery and photographs of the pieces of the victim, they do not flinch; they show no emotion, describing their motivations and deeds with a slow, dull-witted, disjointed precision. A dense hatred of Jews. A vapidly deluded intelligence. Total confidence in Germany, soon to conquer Switzerland, making the Canton of Vaud the Northern Province, with Fernand Ischi as its Prefect. "Gauleiter!" corrects Ischi, drawing himself up.

It emerges from all the interrogations that the example was intended, premeditated, and that they claimed responsibility for it. Fernand Ischi repeated several times: "Germany will get us out of this fix. All of you will have to pay for this, before long."

The five sentences are severe. Prison in all cases.

A life sentence for Fernand Ischi, the ringleader and instigator of the crime.

Life for Robert Marmier and Fritz Joss.

Twenty years for Georges Ballotte, a minor – aged nineteen at the time of the crime.

Just fifteen years for Max Marmier, considered less responsible.

Seeing that the vice was closing on him, Pastor Philippe Lugrin fled to Germany with the help of the diplomatic services of the Reich. He would spend three years there in various translation and espionage services, until he was arrested in Frankfurt in 1945 by the American army, which sentenced him to fifteen years in prison, but then handed him over to the Swiss. The obsessively anti-Semitic theologian would appear before the court in Moudon in 1947 and receive a twenty-year sentence. He served two thirds of his time and came out more ardent than ever, virulent in the density of his hatred.

One day in the summer of 1964, recognizing him at a café table in the old quarter of Lausanne, abandoning all discretion, I decide to sit opposite him and scrutinize him with intense curiosity. I cannot be mistaken. I have seen him only in photographs, but this is him all right, the fearsome Lugrin, sitting by himself just a few inches away. I stare at him; he stares back with the wary, arrogant gaze of a man always ready with a reply and prepared to make his escape. Deep-blue eyes. Angelic. Features unmarked by prison. High forehead. Long, narrow nose. Little round spectacles, whose metal rims frame the brilliant blue eyes that still gaze back at me. A man of God? A man of Satan. The demon has confused the bearings, distorted the aims, invested and perverted the remaining fire in this dead soul.

"You are Pastor Lugrin," I say.

He makes as if to retreat, then stiffens and answers: "Philippe Lugrin. What of it?"

The tone is cutting, the eyes hard; he lowers his head as if to charge, and I get a better view of the smooth, unyielding forehead, the hair, or what is left of it, pasted down with bluish brilliantine. The radiance of that head, almost phosphorescent in the gloom of the café.

"So nothing. I wanted to see at close range the pastor responsible for Arthur Bloch's murder."

"You think you can intimidate me, young fellow, with ancient history!"

He belches, ready to continue. Goes on the offensive:

"You think you can shame me with the business of that Jew? I regret only one thing, mark this well. It is that I didn't bring others to my friends' attention. My *friends*, do you hear!"

He has sat bolt upright on his chair, head high, his tone biting.

I had not at all expected this encounter; mere chance had put me in the presence of this madman. I move to another table without taking my eyes off the individual who is beginning to act on me like a malign magnet. And suddenly a realization: there is such a thing as total depravity, pure in its filth, white-hot on its ruins, and it is a kind of damnation. The dreadfully blinkered man who pursues his absurd dream a few feet away no longer answers to any human authority; he answers to God.

At that moment something said by Jankélévitch comes back to me: "The unprecedented responsibility that is ours, possessing a soul that lives after us, for all eternity..." How can the soul of the person I have just encountered live on? An untroubled, violent little man with small, gleaming spectacles, bent from the outset on hatred of God's creature.

I left the café astonished, thinking of Payerne, where I was born, where I spent my childhood, of Ischi, of his followers and of Lugrin, whom I abandon to his rage. But I have seen Lugrin; it is a sight that leaves one soiled; I must make the effort to put him in his evil place. And all the time I am walking, as I try to lose sight of him, some particularly grave words come to mind: "Do you know this man?" "No, I do not know him. I have never seen him." "Think! You are quite certain you do not know this man?" "No, I do not know him."

As if, already, the dread of seeing him again gripped and distressed me.

16

Monday 27 April 1942, 8 a.m., the Jewish cemetery in Berne. Arthur Bloch's remains are to be buried on a bare little path, about twenty yards from his father's grave. The entire community is there. Its members have come from Basle, Zurich, Fribourg, Vevey, Lausanne, Geneva, Yverdon, Avenches and Payerne: acquaintances and strangers, often friends, sometimes cousins and distant relatives wishing to rally round Myria Bloch and her daughters. To come together, strengthening their bonds in sadness and fear. At 8:30, when Rabbi Messinger begins to speak, the tiny cemetery is crowded as the wind blows up from the River Aar, and tits chirp, hopping from branch to branch of the little elms and the cedars. The weather is fine; it is cool, the air is from the Aar...

Rabbi Messinger recalls what a good man Arthur Bloch was. His love of his family. The humanity that emanated from his words and deeds. And that he had been a Swiss soldier. His refusal to leave this country for the United States, to follow part of his family that emigrated when war broke out. He was a just man, says the Rabbi. And it is this just man, as in ancient times, who has been sacrificed.

Georges Brunschwig's speech is more explicit. He denounces the running sore of racism, and sees Arthur Bloch's murder as a historical and political crime. President of the Jewish community in Berne, Georges Brunschwig spent his childhood in the region of Payerne; he is himself the son of a cattle-dealer from Avenches. He knows what he is talking about when he denounces persecution.

But just then a strange phenomenon occurs. As Brunschwig is speaking, describing the war, Hitler's advancing armies and the threat to exterminate all European Jewry, it seems as if the little cemetery from which these words are ascending detaches itself and for a moment travels back four thousand years into the past, far from the horror, and bathed in a cool, musical light that mitigates and uplifts the tragic scene. And when the Kaddish is recited in fervent, resonant tones, it seems as if the human voice is taken up in God, the witness of these fresh trials and this abode in a barbarous world.

God, once again his people's only guide through a forbidding desert.

The little Jewish cemetery in Berne, that morning a small island of ancestral soil, a moment of grace detached from a world where Aryan rule is bloodily imposed. A narrow patch of land engorged with age-old faith, a faith under threat, wounded and then revivified by the words of the Kaddish recited for Arthur Bloch, and hearts bleed, and injustice bows down our families in Alsace, Hungary and Poland, and one of our own is slaughtered, mutilated and cut up thirty miles from this holy place, O lamentable destiny of our people, a destiny hard to bear. That morning, in the Jewish cemetery in the city of Berne, very near and far from Adolf Hitler's Europe, the martyred body of Arthur Bloch sows both strength and panic in the hearts of all those gathered around his closed grave.

The following year Myria Bloch places a slab over the grave. Contrary to the custom of the Berne community, and against Rabbi Messinger's advice, she has an inscription carved into the cold sandstone:

GOTT WEISS WARUM
[God Knows Why]

The ironic expression of her confidence in, and distrust of, the Almighty's decisions. And that darkness prevails. And that any human understanding, acceptance, knowledge or acknowledgement is for ever impossible.

Myria Bloch would die five years after the murder of her husband and be buried at his side. Patronymic engraved on the slab, with the dates, and Dreyfus, her maiden name. Dead of sadness. And of utter despair. Myria Bloch lost her mind. Absence, dementia. Nothing can be explained, nothing is ever clear to one who has recognized, once and for all, all the injustice done to a living soul. Without reason. Without any purpose. Myria Bloch dies insane, but of grief. And this grief is the barrier. Jankélévitch's "imprescriptible". I reflect on this age-old injustice, and on the example of Arthur Bloch. I encounter the same barrier. A dense refusal in the depths of the void, about which God is silent, or knows and decides, while the axe of the evildoers, the fire of the ovens, condemn us to night and to ashes.

But then again another strange phenomenon occurs. For the old writer who witnessed this story as a young boy sometimes wakens in the night, obsessed and scarred. He takes himself for the child he once was, who asked his family questions. He used to wonder where was the man who had been murdered and dismembered near his home. He used to wonder if he would come back. And what welcome he would receive.

"Is it true this evening that he wanders about?"

"You mean Arthur Bloch," they answer him very quietly. Arthur Bloch is not spoken of. Arthur Bloch, that was before. An old story. A dead story.

But a voice will not be silent in the old man-child's dream.

"So that was before? And it is now?"

Arthur Bloch, the wandering Jew, because he knows no rest beneath the slab that reads *Gott weiss warum.*

Arthur Bloch, who at this moment knows, the absolute God who knows, while we do not know. Arthur Bloch of the dark barrier under the snow. Or under the ashes of time. Because of insults, contempt, the gas chambers, the swastika, the desolation of the hills of Auschwitz and Payerne, the shame of Nazism at Treblinka and in the pig towns on the Broye. It is all a wound. It is all Golgotha. And redemption is so remote. But can there be a resurrection? Pity, God, by the pink of the open belly. Pity by the crown of thorns and the barbed wire of the camps. Have pity, Lord, on our crimes. Lord, have pity on us.